TAKA-CHAN AND I

Taka-chan and I

A Dog's Journey to Japan

by Runcible as told to
Betty Jean Lifton

photographs by Eikoh Hosoe

The New York Review Children's Collection
New York

THIS IS A NEW YORK REVIEW BOOK
PUBLISHED BY THE NEW YORK REVIEW OF BOOKS
435 Hudson Street, New York, NY 10014
www.nyrb.com

Library of Congress Cataloging-in-Publication Data

Lifton, Betty Jean.
Taka-chan and I : a dog's journey to Japan / by Betty Jean Lifton ; photographs by
Eikoh Hosoe.
p. cm. — (New York Review books children's collection)
Summary: Runcible the weimaraner digs a hole in the sand, from Cape Cod all the
way to Japan, where he meets a little girl held captive by a dragon and helps her to
find the most loyal person in Japan.
ISBN 978-1-59017-502-6 (alk. paper)
[1. Adventure and adventurers—Fiction. 2. Weimaraner (Dog breed)—Fiction. 3.
Dogs—Fiction. 4. Dragons—Fiction. 5. Japan—Fiction.] I. Hosoe, Eiko, 1933– ill. II.
Title.
PZ7.L6225Tak 2012
[Fic]—dc23
2011029636

ISBN 978-1-59017-502-6

Cover design by Katy Homans

Printed in the United States of America on acid-free paper

1 3 5 7 9 10 8 6 4 2

For Minako and Shiro—
who were Runcible's friends.

Call me Runcible. That is what my master calls me—and that is what Taka-chan called me from the time we first met.

I want to tell you about Taka-chan, how I found her on the other side of the earth. It is a strange story, almost like a dream, but who is to say what is a dream and what is real?

It all began when I was digging a hole in the sand on the beach near my Cape Cod home. The hole kept getting deeper and deeper until I saw a long, dark tunnel stretching out before me.

At first it was wonderful following that mysterious tunnel through the darkness. But when I became tired and tried to turn around, I discovered the hole was too narrow. I could only go straight ahead.

It may have been hours, days, years, that I went on, sometimes sliding, sometimes falling great distances. I could not tell. But finally I became so weak and hungry, I could hardly take another step. It is the end, I thought. I shall never see my master or my food pan again.

I was about to lie down and give up forever, when I saw a small ray of light just beyond. . . .

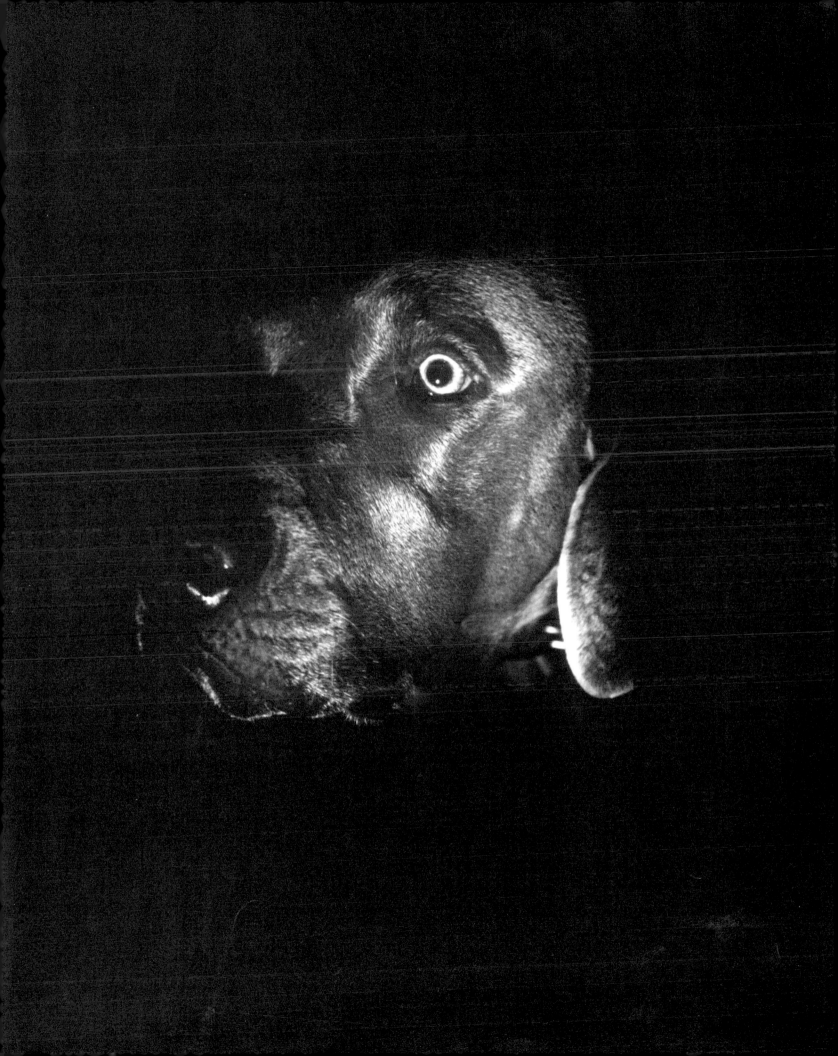

I managed to crawl up to it and poke my head out. Two dark, shining eyes peered into mine. It was then that I first saw Taka-chan. She was bending down over the hole, and in the mist which hung over that unknown beach to which I had come, she seemed like a princess waiting for me.

"I am Runcible," I said, almost with my last breath.

But her voice was filled with fear. "Whoever you are, go back where you came from," she cried.

"I cannot," I said weakly. "I have traveled such a long way. I must have food and rest."

"Oh, do not seek it *here!*" she pleaded, her lovely brown eyes filling with tears.

"Where am I?" I barked.

"On a lonely seashore of Japan," she replied. "You must flee for your life."

"But why?" I asked.

"I cannot tell you," she said. "Please just go."

"I haven't the strength to go farther," I said desperately. "Please let me stay with you for just one night."

Taka-chan looked at me closely. My eyes were red and swollen, and my ears twitched uncontrollably.

"All right," she said sympathetically. "Since you are a foreigner, perhaps he will not harm you."

But she did not say who *he* was. And I was too tired to care.

I followed Taka-chan across the beach and up a low hill, past twisted pine trees and tropical shrubs. Her house loomed before us like an enchanted palace rising out of the twilight. What could happen to anyone in such a beautiful place? I thought.

Taka-chan entered the house cautiously after removing her shoes. My nails made a clacking sound next to the soft padding of her bare feet on the wooden corridor. I thought she was going to hide me in a special place, and so I was amazed when I suddenly found myself in a bath.

"*He* will not want you getting his palace dirty," she said.

And then she scrubbed and massaged me so gently that even I, a famous bath hater, could not help but enjoy the warm clean glow I felt when it was all over.

Then she led me into her room. Perhaps I should have noticed then how strange it was that the table was already set for two, with hot steaming fish and rice upon it, as if my arrival were expected. But I saw no one except Taka-chan.

I was almost too exhausted to eat. Taka-chan fed me tenderly with her own chopsticks.

When we were finished, Taka-chan took two beds out of the closet, and rolled them down next to each other on the floor.

"Sleep well, Runcible," she whispered with a loving smile. "Try not to hear anything. But if you do," she added nervously, "I beg you, go back to sleep."

My eyes closed while she was speaking. I fell into a deep, dreamless slumber from which I might not have awakened for days, if a booming voice, like thunder, had not roared through the room. The very floor beneath me shook as if there were an earthquake. I woke trembling with fear.

"Taka-chan!" I cried. "What is it?"

She sat up in bed and lit the candle. I could see her face was pale with fright. "He knows you are here," she said. "He wants to see you immediately."

"Who is *he*?" I asked.

"The Black Dragon of the Sea," she replied with a trembling voice. "Last month he kidnapped me from my fishing village and imprisoned me here in his palace."

"You're a prisoner!" I cried in astonishment. And truly in the flickering candlelight, Taka-chan was beginning to look like a fairy princess who had been captured by an evil dragon.

"But why is he holding you here?" I asked.

"I don't know," said Taka-chan, beginning to weep. "His dragon guards leave me food, like the dinner we had, but won't let me escape."

"Don't worry, Taka-chan," I said bravely, although I was really very worried myself. "Perhaps there is some way I can rescue you. Come, dry your tears, and take me to the Black Dragon."

However, as I followed Taka-chan up the dark stairway, my heart was pounding rapidly. The wind rattled the shutters, and the steps creaked under our feet. I had promised to protect Taka-chan, but who was going to protect me?

At the top of the
stairs, there was a
door with no handle.
Taka-chan slid it
open, and we peered
inside.
"Come forward,"
said a fierce voice.
We walked with
pounding hearts
to where the voice
came from.

There by the dim candlelight we could see the Black Dragon perched up on the wall. He was a most ferocious looking creature. His thick scaly body was as black as the night, from the tip of his long hooked claws to the top of his two sharp horns.

"What are you doing in my palace?" he boomed at me.

"Pardon me," I said as humbly as I could. "I was digging a hole on the other side of the world, and I came out here."

He looked at me with disbelief. I couldn't blame him, for I could hardly believe it myself.

"Then you are a foreign dog," he said thoughtfully. "You must have magic powers since no one else has ever been able to find my palace."

"That's right," I said quickly. Already a plan was forming in my mind. "I have come to find out why you are holding Taka-chan a prisoner."

"I have good reason," roared the Black Dragon. "Taka-chan's father is a fisherman, and Japanese fishermen are no longer loyal to us dragons."

"No longer loyal?" I asked, quite confused. "What do you mean?"

"In the old days the people of Taka-chan's village used to reward the dragons who protected their fishing boats in the storms," he replied. "They left rice balls and rice wine for us on the shore. But now no one leaves us anything. I am going to hold Taka-chan until her father and the other fishermen are loyal to us dragons again."

"But Taka-chan is not to blame," I replied hotly. "I demand that you free her this instant!"

"What! You dare give me orders?" bellowed the dragon.

"I do!" I replied, although my legs were shaking under me.

And then, surprisingly enough, the dragon became quite gentle. "You have courage," he said, with a little chuckle. "Next to people with loyalty, I like people with courage. Therefore, I will let Taka-chan go"—he paused and then continued—" if you can fulfill a task I give you."

"I will do it!" I barked, for I was sure that nothing would be too difficult to do for Taka-chan.

"Listen carefully," said the Black Dragon. "It is almost dawn. By sundown of this very day you must find the most loyal person in Japan, and lay a white flower at his feet. If you can do this, I will disappear from this palace, and Taka-chan will be free."

"I'll sniff out that loyal person easily," I barked, although I knew I had never sniffed out anything more difficult than my bones in the past. "But since I am a stranger here," I added, "I would like to take Taka-chan with me on my search."

The Black Dragon thought this over for a while. "I grant your request," he said finally. "But remember, if you fail in your task by sundown, I shall get both of you wherever you are—and you'll be my prisoners for the rest of your miserable lives!"

And this time he emitted a most hideous laugh. Taka-chan and I crept out before he was finished.

On the stairway outside, I asked Taka-chan if she had any idea where the most loyal person could be.

She shook her head sadly. "But Tokyo is our largest city," she said. "Almost everyone lives there, even the Emperor. So maybe the most loyal person does too!"

"Then to Tokyo!" I barked. "To Tokyo, right away!"

"To Tokyo!" repeated Taka-chan, tears of gratitude shining in her lovely eyes.

By the time we made our plans, the sun had come up. In the garden a pure white lily was just opening its petals to the new day.

"We shall lay this flower at the most loyal person's feet," said Taka-chan.

I had the feeling that the flower was pleased to be chosen. Taka-chan wrapped it in a large handkerchief, along with some rice balls for our lunch, and we set off.

There was only one road leading from the house.

"In Japan all roads lead to Tokyo," said Taka-chan, as we started hopefully down it. Fortunately, neither of us knew, while passing the peaceful little rice paddies and vegetable fields, how many difficulties lay ahead.

On the way we saw six stone statues.

"They are The Six Jizo," said Taka-chan. "They protect children and travelers. Oh Runcible, do you think they will help us while we are in Tokyo?"

"I hope so," I replied. "We can use all the help we can get."

It must have been about noon when we reached Tokyo. It was a huge city. Never had I seen so many people all crowded together into one place. Everyone was hurrying by so quickly it was impossible to ask anyone about the most loyal person.

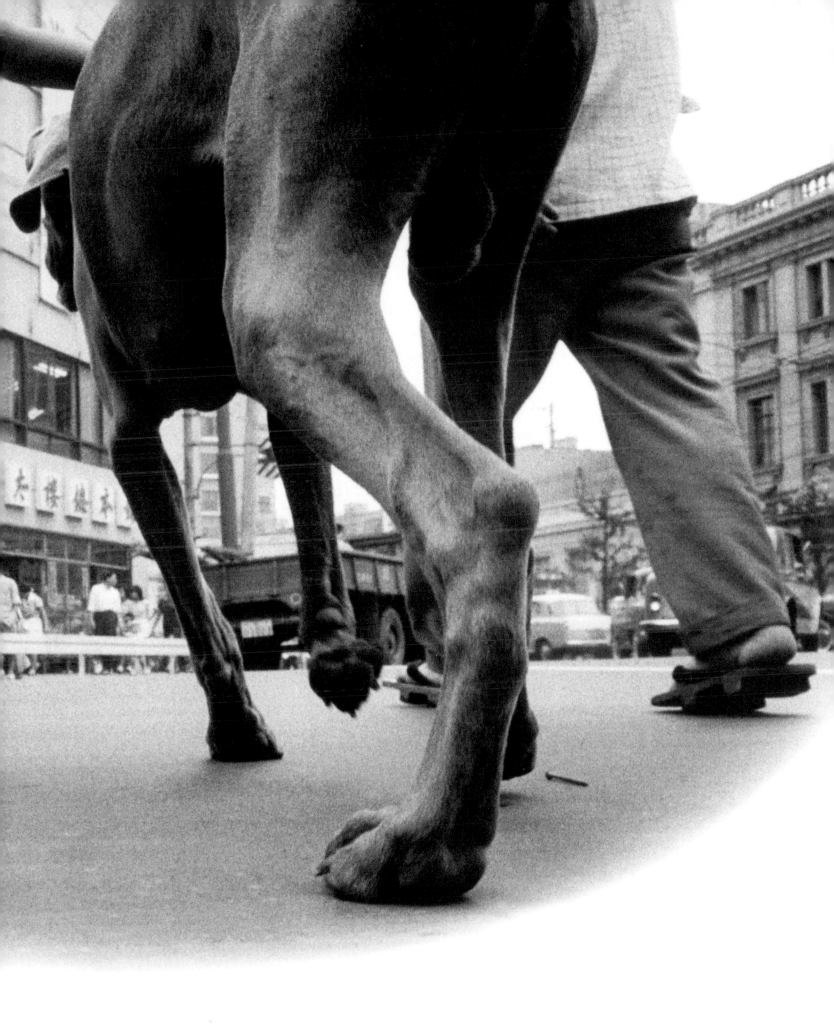

Finally we came to a pet shop. A cockatoo was sunning himself outside.

"Pardon me," I barked eagerly. "The Black Dragon is going to get us if we don't...."

"The Black Dragon!" shrieked the cockatoo. "EEEEEE, the Black Dragon!" And the poor bird flapped about so frantically he could not utter another sound.

Feeling sorry for him, Taka-chan and I continued on our way.

But after we had gone just a short distance, something terrible happened. Taka-chan and I lost each other in the crowd. When I turned around, Taka-chan wasn't there.

"Taka-chan! Taka-chan!" I barked. But she was nowhere in sight. I raced madly along the streets looking for her. "Oh what will become of poor Taka-chan and the white flower without me!" I moaned.

I was so busy worrying about them, I almost forgot I was all alone on the other side of the world. And that I had only about four hours until sundown.

I must have spent at least an hour wandering through those unknown streets. At times I felt I was going in circles, and the unfamiliar smells made my head reel. But then, like a miracle, I found myself in an enormous park. In the distance I could see the faint outlines of an exquisite palace, much grander than the Black Dragon's.

It must be the Emperor's palace, I thought. Surely the Emperor will know who the most loyal person in his kingdom is. And perhaps he will know how I can find Taka-chan too.

I was so excited I ran through the outer gates and into the inner gardens, until I came to a wooden barrier just in front of the palace door.

I had no idea how one addresses anyone so grand as an Emperor, so I called timidly at first. " Oh, Mr. Emperor, sir, please let me in."

However, the Emperor did not seem to hear.

I tried again. " Oh Mr. Emperor, sir, can you tell me where I can find the most loyal person in Japan?"

Still there was no answer.

Perhaps the Emperor is taking a nap, I thought. I will look for another entrance under his window.

I was searching through the grounds along the palace moat when I came upon two young swans.

"The Emperor does not need any more horses," honked one.

"I am a dog, not a horse," I replied indignantly. I added a sharp "bow wow wow" to prove it.

"In Japan dogs say 'wan wan wan,'" said the other crossly.

"But in any language, dogs are not allowed on the palace grounds," snorted the first.

"I am here on a special mission," I explained importantly. "I am looking for the most loyal person in the Emperor's kingdom."

"Only a mad dog would look for a loyal person here anymore," screeched the first.

"A mad dog. Mad dog! Mad dog!" shrieked the second.

I left with a heavy heart. "Well, at least I will be loyal to Taka-chan," I told myself. "I will keep on searching."

Only two hours until sunset. By now my legs were heavy with fatigue, and I was weak from hunger. I thought longingly of the rice balls in Taka-chan's kerchief. Would I ever see Taka-chan and the white flower and the rice balls again? Or would I die of loneliness and hunger right here in the streets of Tokyo?

I was almost wishing I had never dug that hole, when suddenly the door of a little shop slid open and a hand offered me some raw fish. It was delicious. I felt strong again. Could this man be one of The Six Jizo in disguise?

I trotted eagerly down the street again. Soon I sniffed something familiar, and following the scent, I found myself in a zoo. There I met a friendly old deer.

"Pardon me, Mr. Deer, sir," I said. "My life depends on my finding the most loyal person in Japan by sundown. Do you know who he is?"

Much to my amazement, the old deer answered gently, "Of course. Everyone knows that the most loyal person is Hachiko."

"Hachiko!" I repeated, hardly able to believe my good fortune. "And do you know where he is?" I asked breathlessly.

"Of course," said the deer. "He's sitting loyally in front of Shibuya station waiting for a certain train."

"Oh, how do I get to Shibuya station?" I barked.

"It's easy, my son," said the old deer. "You just follow your nose two blocks as the wind goes, turn right at the fish store, then left at the noodle shop, and you'll see the station straight ahead."

I wagged my tail thankfully. And then I had another question since the old deer was so wise. "Oh, Mr. Deer, sir," I said. "If you lost a little girl and a white flower, where would you go to find them?"

"I'd go to the place where I last saw them, of course," said the deer.

"But, of course," I cried, already on my way.

I raced all the way back to that petshop, my heart pounding, my ears flying, my paws barely touching the ground. And there was Taka-chan waiting for me, right in front of the cockatoo's cage.

"Oh, Runcible, I just knew you'd come back and find me!" she cried joyously.

"I've also found the most loyal person," I barked proudly. "Come on, Taka-chan, follow me!"

There were just a few minutes to go. Taka-chan and I ran breathlessly through the streets, past the zoo, then two blocks as the wind blows, right at the fish store, left at the noodle shop, and there was the station straight ahead. But I didn't see anyone sitting in front of it. All I could see was the sun getting ready to set in the western sky.

For the first time I felt my courage fail. Taka-chan and I were doomed. "Hachiko's not here," I told her as bravely as I could. "And our time is almost up."

"Hachiko!" cried Taka-chan excitedly, as if she hadn't heard the rest of what I had said. "I should have thought of Loyal Hachiko. There he is over there!"

I looked to where she pointed, but all I could see was a large bronze dog sitting on a pedestal in front of the station.

"My mother told me all about Hachiko when I was little," said Taka-chan. And then she told me the story as she remembered it.

It seems that many years ago Hachiko used to follow his master to this train station in the morning when he went to work and wait for him in the evening to return. But one evening Hachiko's master did not appear. He had taken ill and died at the office that day; but poor Hachiko had no way of knowing.

And so he waited loyally until the last train that night, and the next day he was still waiting. And the next day, and the next. Finally people began bringing him food, but no one could ever persuade him to go home alone.

For ten years Hachiko waited for his master who was never to come. When he died, this statue was placed in the same spot so that he could continue to wait there loyally forever after.

There were tears in Taka-chan's and my eyes when she finished her story.

The sun was setting as she placed the white flower at Hachiko's feet. I think I saw Hachiko nod, as if he were happy we had succeeded in our task.

Then Taka-chan and I hurried back to the Black Dragon's palace. When we got there, the dragon was already gone. Only the empty wall where he had sat remained.

There was a message from him on the floor for Taka-chan. He would give his palace and everything in it to her family if they would leave rice balls and rice wine on the shore once again for the dragons.

By now Taka-chan and I were so tired we just fell into bed. But I could not sleep. I lay awake thinking of Loyal Hachiko and his faithfulness to his master.

Finally I got up and opened the wooden shutters a crack, and peered out into the darkness, far beyond the sea. Hachiko would not have left his master for so long. I knew then it was my duty as a loyal dog to return home.

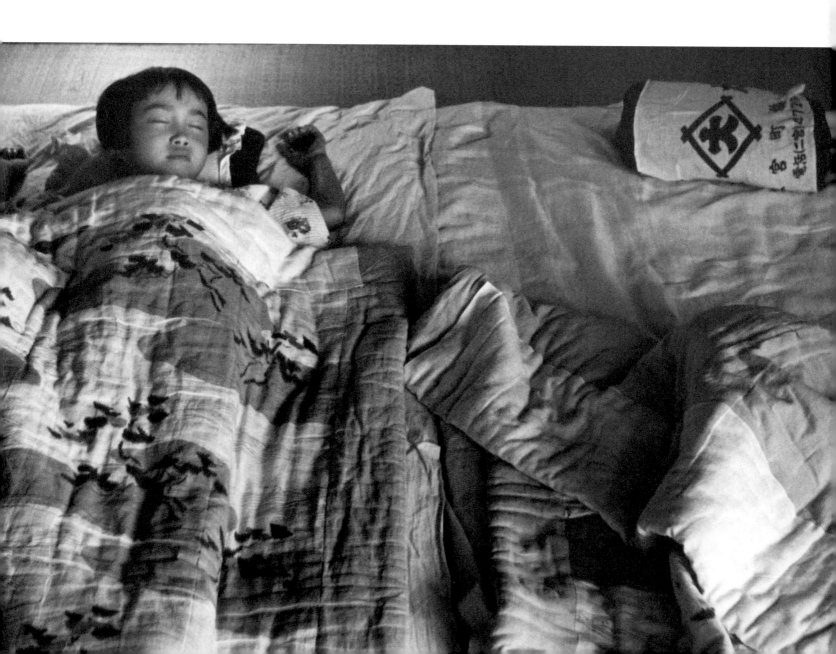

It wasn't easy to tell Taka-chan the next morning. I could see she was fighting to hold back the tears. "I was hoping you would stay in Japan and be my dog," she said simply, as we walked down the little hill to the beach. Then we tried to talk and laugh as if it weren't for the last time.

We found the hole still there, waiting for me. I knew it was meant to lead me back to the land where I belonged.

"I'll never forget you, Runcible," Taka-chan said.

"And I'll never forget you, Taka-chan," I said, pressing her hand with my paw. "But compared to Loyal Hachiko, I'm afraid I'm not much of a dog."

"Oh, don't say that," she protested in a choked voice. "Even Hachiko could not have been a more loyal friend in freeing me from the Black Dragon."

Her words meant more to me than she could ever understand.

"Good-by, Taka-chan," I said. "Don't get lost on the way home." And I added a brave "wan wan wan" for her sake.

"Good-by, Runcible. Sayonara. You get home safely, too. But come back to me someday."

"Yes, I'll come back...someday," I cried. And then to hide my tears, I jumped quickly into the hole.

Many years have passed since then. But at night, when I close my eyes by my master's bed, I can still see that misty little beach where Taka-chan and I once walked. It seems so real that I can almost touch the sand with my paws and hear her voice in the wind.

There were those dogs who told me on my return that it was all a dream, that there was no such hole as I have told you about, no Black Dragon, no Loyal Hachiko, no Taka-chan.

But I ask you again—who is to say what is a dream, and what is real?

BETTY JEAN LIFTON discovered a passion for Japanese culture and folklore while living in Japan with her husband, the psychiatrist Robert Jay Lifton, in the early 1960s. Out of that interest came many children's books, including *Kap the Kappa, Joji and the Dragon, The Rice-cake Rabbit,* and *The Dwarf Pine Tree.* After the publication of *Taka-chan and I*, Lifton and Eikoh Hosoe collaborated on three more books: *A Dog's Guide to Tokyo, A Place Called Hiroshima,* and *Return to Hiroshima.* In 1975 she published *Twice Born: Memoirs of an Adopted Daughter,* which marked the start of her second career as an adoption writer, counselor, and adoptee-rights advocate. She died in 2010, after many years living in New York City, Cambridge, Massachusetts, and Wellfleet, Cape Cod.

EIKOH HOSOE is one of Japan's preemenant photographers. His work can be found in the collections of the Museum of Modern Art, New York, the Victoria and Albert Museum, the Georges Pompidou Center, the Smithsonian, and the Art Institute of Chicago, among other museums. In 2010 and 2011 Theatre of Memory, a retrospective exhibit of Hosoe's dance photography, was shown at the Japan Foundation, Cologne and the Art Gallery of New South Wales.

RUNCIBLE was the youngest in a litter of eleven Weimaraner puppies. He was born in Framingham, Massachusetts, and at the age of seven weeks was adopted by Betty Jean Lifton. It was from Mrs. Lifton that Runcible developed his nose for literature. He began digging up the material for this book during a two-year stay in Japan. Runcible is a firm believer in international understanding. "The world would be a better place if more dogs would travel," he says.

Runcible and Eikoh Hosoe met one day when the photographer was walking on a lonely beach in Japan. Mr. Hosoe couldn't believe his eyes when he saw a dog coming right out of the ground, but before Runcible's departure from Japan the two had a long talk and Runcible told Mr. Hosoe about his adventure.